Amelia Bedelia Storybook Treasury

Text copyright © 2002, 2008, 2010, and 2016 by Herman S. Parish III

Illustrations copyright © 2002, 2008, 2010, and 2016 by Lynn Sweat

Amelia Bedelia is a registered trademark of Peppermint Partners LLC.

Manufactured in China. For information address HarperCollins Children's Books,
a division of HarperCollins Publishers, 195 Broadway, New York, NY 10007.

www.harpercollinschildrens.com

Watercolors and a black pen were used to create the full-color art.
The text type is Times Roman.

Library of Congress Cataloging-in-Publication Data is available.

ISBN 978-0-06-246908-3 (trade ed.)

Calling Doctor Amelia Bedelia Library of Congress number: 2002017510
Amelia Bedelia and the Cat Library of Congress number: 2007019461
Amelia Bedelia Bakes Off Library of Congress number: 2009021397

16 17 18 19 SCP 10 9 8 7 6 5 4 3 2 1

Greenwillow Books

Ameli
Bedeli

Storybook Treas

By **Herman Parish** ◆ Pictures by

 Greenwillow Books, *An Imprint of Har*

Contents

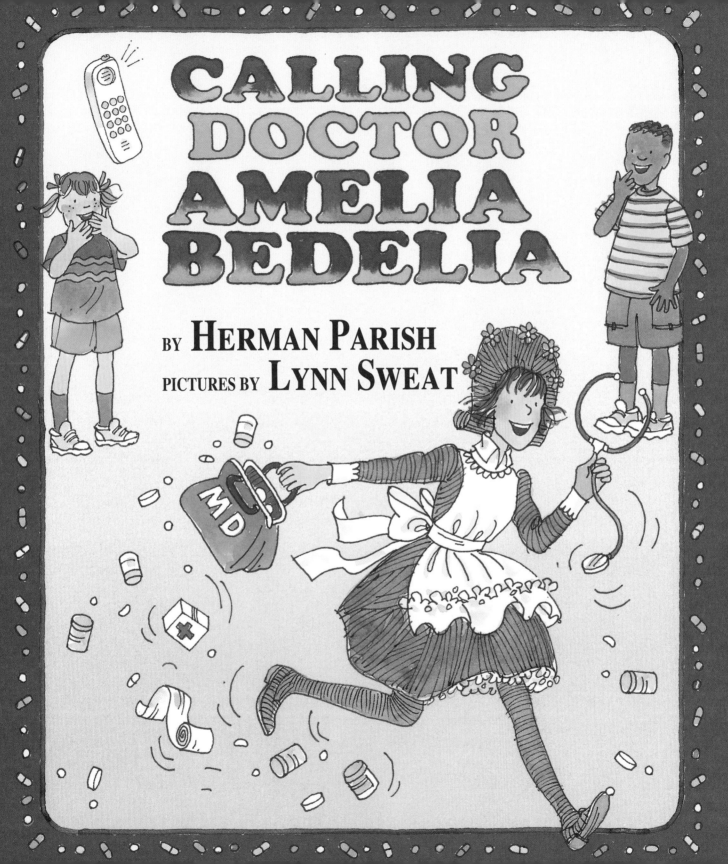

CALLING DOCTOR AMELIA BEDELIA

BY **HERMAN PARISH**

PICTURES BY **LYNN SWEAT**

It was a hot day in August.

Mr. Rogers was even hotter.

"Amelia Bedelia," yelled Mr. Rogers,

"what are you doing?"

"What's wrong?" said Amelia Bedelia.

"You said it was hot enough to . . ."

"Stop!" said Mr. Rogers.

"I said it was hot enough to fry an egg

on the sidewalk. Not on my car."

"Well," said Amelia Bedelia,

"you should be glad.

I would never fry your eggs

on a dirty old sidewalk."

"Forget about eggs,"

said Mr. Rogers.

"You will be late

for your appointment

with Dr. Horton.

Jump in the car."

"Yes, sir," said Amelia Bedelia.

She bounced up and down

on her seat.

"Sit still," said Mr. Rogers.

"Good," said Amelia Bedelia.

"It wasn't easy

to jump in your car."

Mr. Rogers shook his head.

"What kind of doctor is Dr. Horton?"

he asked.

"The best kind," said Amelia Bedelia.

"She is a very good doctor."

"Of course," said Mr. Rogers.

"I mean, who does Dr. Horton treat?"

"Everyone," said Amelia Bedelia.

"And she treats good boys and girls

to ice cream."

They arrived at Dr. Horton's office.

Mr. Rogers took out a bottle.

"What are those pills?"

asked Amelia Bedelia.

"They are for a headache,"

said Mr. Rogers.

"Why do you want a headache?"

asked Amelia Bedelia.

"I have a headache now,"

said Mr. Rogers.

"Then why do you want

another one?"

asked Amelia Bedelia.

"I don't," said Mr. Rogers.

"In fact, I am getting rid

of my biggest headache.

Good-bye!"

"Good-bye!"

said Amelia Bedelia.

"Thanks for the ride.

And I hope you feel better."

"Thank you," said Mr. Rogers.

"Call me when you are done."

Amelia Bedelia opened the door

to Dr. Horton's office.

It was a lot noisier than usual.

"Amelia Bedelia!" said Nurse Ames.

"You are a sight for sore eyes."

"How terrible," said Amelia Bedelia.

"I am sorry that your eyes hurt."

"My eyes are fine," said Nurse Ames.

"But I am up to my eyeballs

in patients.

Dr. Horton had to visit the hospital.

Would you give me a hand

until she gets back?"

"No," said Amelia Bedelia.

"Both my hands are attached to me.

But I would be glad to help you."

Right then the telephone rang.

"Hello, this is Dr. Horton's office,"

said Amelia Bedelia.

"This is Mrs. Bender," said a woman.

"I am calling because I've got hives."

"That's great!" said Amelia Bedelia.

"I'll bet you have honey."

"Don't call me 'honey,'"

said Mrs. Bender.

"Do you know what it means

to have hives?"

"I sure do—honey!"

said Amelia Bedelia.

"Stop calling me 'honey!'"

said Mrs. Bender.

"I am coming down

to see Dr. Horton right now."

"Good," said Amelia Bedelia.

"Please bring us some honey."

Mrs. Bender hung up on her.

"Guess what?" said Amelia Bedelia.

"Mrs. Bender is coming to see us."

"Oh, my," said Nurse Ames.

"Mrs. Bender is a pain in the neck.

  But her heart is in the right place."

"Wow!" said Amelia Bedelia.

"It would be terrible

  if her heart were down in her foot."

"This is April," said Nurse Ames.

"She is a little scared.

 Will you take her temperature?"

"I will try," said Amelia Bedelia.

"Give it a shot," said Nurse Ames.

"A shot!" wailed April.

"Don't worry," said Nurse Ames.

"It is just a thermometer.

Amelia Bedelia, will you tell me

the temperature in three minutes?"

"I don't have a watch,"

said Amelia Bedelia.

"Look out the window,"

said Nurse Ames.

"The bank across the street

has a big clock."

Brrrrrr-ING!

Amelia Bedelia was busier than ever.

She answered call after call after call.

"I hear a ringing in my ears."

"A ringing? Maybe you should answer the doorbell."

"My nose hurts, on the bridge."

"Well, get off that bridge!"

"I've caught some kind of bug."

"I hope you let it go. Bugs can bite."

"Oh, Amelia Bedelia," said Nurse Ames.

"Don't forget about the temperature."

Amelia Bedelia ran to the window.

"It says ninety-eight degrees."

"Fine," said Nurse Ames.

"Ninety-eight is normal."

"Yes," said Amelia Bedelia,

"that is normal for August."

"For August?" said Nurse Ames.

"Don't you mean for April?"

 Finally, April smiled.

A boy came into the office.

"Excuse me," he said.

"I am here for a test."

"Then you must be lost,"

said Amelia Bedelia.

"You have to go to school

to take a test."

"I am here for a blood test,"

 said the boy.

"Blood test?" asked Amelia Bedelia.

"What kind of crazy test is that?

 True or false?"

"I wish it were," said the boy.

"Well," said Amelia Bedelia,

"let's give it a try.

   True or false: Do you have blood?"

"True," he said.

"Of course I have blood."

"Then you pass," said Amelia Bedelia.

"What if I didn't have blood?"

   asked the boy.

"Then you would pass out,"

   said Amelia Bedelia.

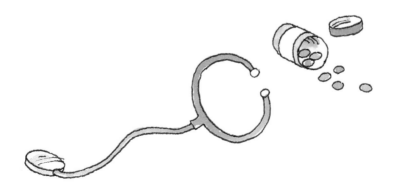

"Hi, Andy," said Nurse Ames.

"We need to draw your blood.

Amelia Bedelia, please take Andy

to the examination room."

"Look at all this blank paper,"

said Amelia Bedelia.

"Andy, why don't you draw

your own blood?"

Amelia Bedelia gave Andy

a big red pen.

He began to draw.

"My mom told me," said Andy,

"that when you draw blood,

I will feel a little stick."

Amelia Bedelia looked all around.

"Here," she said.

"Feel this old ice cream stick."

"Those depress your tongue,"

said Andy.

"Right you are," said Amelia Bedelia.

"A stick without ice cream

would depress anyone's tongue."

"That reminds me,"

said Amelia Bedelia.

She made a phone call.

As soon as she hung up,

the phone rang again.

"Dr. Horton's office,"

said Amelia Bedelia.

"I have a problem," said a man.

"I am a little hoarse."

"A little horse? Hah!"

said Amelia Bedelia.

"You can't fool me.

A pony can't talk."

"I have a frog in my throat,"

the man croaked.

"Yuck!" said Amelia Bedelia.

"Spit it out!"

"Listen to me," he said.

"I'm as sick as a dog."

"Make up your mind,"

said Amelia Bedelia.

"Pony, frog, or dog?

Maybe you should call a vet."

"I am coming down there,"

he said, and hung up.

The phone rang again.

"Dr. Horton's office,"

said Amelia Bedelia.

"Hello, my office," joked Dr. Horton.

"Hi, Dr. Horton," said Amelia Bedelia.

"I have been helping Nurse Ames."

"How nice of you," said Dr. Horton.

"So much has happened,"

said Amelia Bedelia.

"But best of all,

April is normal for August."

"April? August? What?"

said Dr. Horton.

"Then I gave Andy a blood test,"

said Amelia Bedelia.

"You drew Andy's blood?"

asked Dr. Horton.

"No," said Amelia Bedelia.

"Andy drew his own blood.

The table is covered with it."

"What?" shouted Dr. Horton.

"Are you treating my patients?"

"Not yet," said Amelia Bedelia,

"but I will soon."

"Don't tease me," said Dr. Horton.

"I am almost out of patience."

"Oh, no, you're not,"

said Amelia Bedelia.

"Your office is full of patients!"

"I will be right there," said Dr. Horton.

The office door burst open.

"Out of my way!" yelled a woman.

"I am Mrs. Bender.

Just look at my hives!"

"How nice!" said Amelia Bedelia.

"You came to bring us honey!

But first let's take care

of that pain in your neck."

Amelia Bedelia began to wrap

Mrs. Bender in bandages.

But she did not finish the job.

All the patients Amelia Bedelia

had upset on the phone

stormed into the waiting room.

Just then Dr. Horton walked in.

"Calm down," said Dr. Horton.

"I will take care of everyone."

MY THROAT!
OH, MY STOMACH!
MY HEAD ACHES!
MY NOSE HURTS!
STOP THAT RINGING!

Dr. Horton looked

at the crowd in her office.

"Who is first?" she asked.

"Me!" said the delivery man.

"This ice cream is starting to melt."

"What ice cream?" said Dr. Horton.

"Your ice cream," said Amelia Bedelia.

"I told you

I was treating your patients."

Dr. Horton laughed.

"Good for you," she said.

"My patient patients all deserve a treat."

They were enjoying their ice cream

when Mr. Rogers arrived.

"Amelia Bedelia!" said Mr. Rogers.

"I was worried. Why didn't you call?"

"I have been busy,"

said Amelia Bedelia.

"Yes," said Dr. Horton.

"She was a huge help.

And you must be Mr. Rogers."

"Pleased to meet you,"

said Mr. Rogers.

Dr. Horton looked at Mr. Rogers.

"Do you feel okay?" asked Dr. Horton.

"You don't look very good."

"We know that," said Amelia Bedelia.

"But we have gotten used to him."

"Say 'ahhh,'" said Dr. Horton.

"Uh-oh," said Mr. Rogers.

"Not 'uh-oh,'" said Amelia Bedelia.

"Say 'ahhhhhh!' Like this."

"Ah-hah!" said Dr. Horton.

"I knew it. Amelia Bedelia,

take Mr. Rogers home

and get him into bed."

"I am as strong as an ox!"

said Mr. Rogers.

"Yes, dear," said Mrs. Rogers.

"And as stubborn as a mule . . .

with chicken pox."

"Speaking of chickens,"

said Amelia Bedelia,

"here is some homemade

chicken soup."

"Yum!" said Mr. Rogers.

"This hits the spot."

"Which spot?" asked Amelia Bedelia.

"That big spot on your cheek,

or that little spot on your chin,

or maybe the teeny-tiny spot on . . . ?"

"Enough," said Mr. Rogers.

"Okay," said Amelia Bedelia.

"I will go and wash those eggs

off your car."

"Good idea," said Mr. Rogers.

"Put some wax on it, too."

"Sure thing," said Amelia Bedelia.

Amelia Bedelia got a pail

and some water.

And she did not forget the wax.

Amelia Bedelia's All Mixed Up!

Amelia Bedelia is all mixed up! Help her by unscrambling these words. (Hint: Use the pictures to help you figure out the words.)

E G U O T N

TONGUE

G E G

EGG

O E N S

NOSE

C I E   M E R A C

ICE CREAM (2 word

Spot the Difference

These two pictures are not
exactly the same.
Five things from picture #1
are missing from picture #2.
Can you spot them?

Two Ways to Say It!

I've got hives.

I broke out in spots because I'm allergic to something.

I have a frog in my throat.

I have a lump in my throat.

I am a little horse.

My voice is a little hoarse.

My nose hurts, on the bridge.

The upper part of my nose is hurting.

Amelia Bedelia always takes things literally, and that leads to funny misunderstandings. Here are some confusing expressions from *Calling Doctor Amelia Bedelia*. Can you think of any other words or expressions Amelia Bedelia misunderstands in this story?

Would you give me a hand?

Would you help out?

I've caught some kind of bug.

I have an infection or the flu.

She is a pain in the neck.

She's very annoying.

I'm as sick as a dog.

I feel completely miserable.

AMELIA BEDELIA
and the CAT

BY **Herman Parish**
PICTURES BY **Lynn Sweat**

Mrs. Rogers was in a total tizzy.

"I am late for a lunch date," she said.

"But I must find an umbrella before I go.

They say it is going to rain cats and dogs."

"Goody!" said Amelia Bedelia.

"We will get a free pet.

Would you like a dog or a cat?"

"Neither one," said Mrs. Rogers.

"All I want is an umbrella."

"Here you go," said Amelia Bedelia.

She pulled an umbrella out of her purse.

"Why do you keep it in there?" asked Mrs. Rogers.

"Blame Mr. Rogers," said Amelia Bedelia.

"He always tells me to save for a rainy day,

but an umbrella would be more help than money.

Would you like to borrow my rubber boots

and rain hat, too?"

"Save them for next time," said Mrs. Rogers.

"Thanks for lending me your umbrella."

They walked out to the car.

Mrs. Rogers got in.

"I have to go shopping later," said Amelia Bedelia.

"Really?" said Mrs. Rogers. "I may run into you."

"I hope not," said Amelia Bedelia.

"It would hurt if you ran into me."

"I have an idea," said Mrs. Rogers.

"Why don't I give you a lift and drop you in town?"

"I know why not," said Amelia Bedelia.

"It's because I am too heavy for you to lift.

You would drop me before we got to town."

Mrs. Rogers nodded, smiled, and drove away.

Amelia Bedelia walked back to the house.

She stood on the porch and gazed at the clouds.

"Rain cats and dogs," she said to herself.

"The weatherman might be right.

That cloud looks like a dog.

That one looks like a really big cat."

"Yipes!" hollered Amelia Bedelia

as she jumped back in shock.

"That cloud just meowed at me."

Amelia Bedelia looked down,

where the sound had come from.

MEOW... MEOW...

"Hmmm," said Amelia Bedelia.

"I have heard of a plant called a cattail,

but I've never seen a plant with a cat tail."

A kitten peeked out from behind the plant.

"Well, I'll be!" said Amelia Bedelia.

"You are the tiniest kitten I have ever seen."

The kitten leaped out of the flowers.

It walked over to Amelia Bedelia

and rubbed up against her leg.

"Where's your mama?"

asked Amelia Bedelia.

"You are much too little

to be out on your own."

She picked up the kitten.

"You look like a tiny tiger,"

said Amelia Bedelia.

She scratched it between its ears.

The kitten purred and purred.

"You even sound like a tiny tiger,"

said Amelia Bedelia.

"So Tiger is what I'll call you."

She took Tiger into the kitchen.

She poured milk into a saucer.

Tiger lapped it up right away.

"Wow," said Amelia Bedelia.

"You must have been starving."

She offered the kitten

half of her sandwich.

Tiger turned up his nose.

"I need help," said Amelia Bedelia.

"I have never taken care of a cat before."

Amelia Bedelia got out the phone book.

"Aha," she said as she dialed the number.

"These folks know all about animals."

A man answered the phone and said,

"City Zoo, Mr. Lyon speaking."

"This is amazing,"

said Amelia Bedelia.

"I have never spoken with a lion."

"I am not a lion," said Mr. Lyon.

"Of course not," said Amelia Bedelia.

"I am sure that you tell the truth."

"I always do," he said. "May I help you?"

"I hope so," said Amelia Bedelia.

"I've got a very hungry Tiger

 right here in my kitchen."

"Run!" said Mr. Lyon.

"Get out of the house!"

"Calm down," said Amelia Bedelia.

"My Tiger is very happy.

 I just gave him some milk."

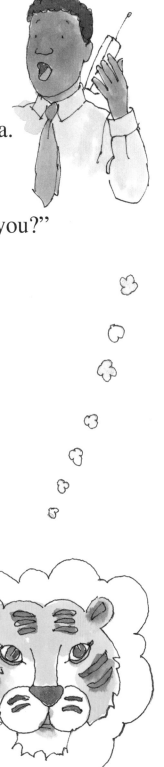

"Milk?" said Mr. Lyon.

"Big cats cat meat."

"You do?" said Amelia Bedelia.

"Not me," said Mr. Lyon.

"I am a vegetarian."

"You can't be," said Amelia Bedelia.

"You're a lion."

"I am not lying!" said Mr. Lyon.

"I hope not," said Amelia Bedelia.

"I have a hungry Tiger in my lap."

"Ha!" said Mr. Lyon.

"I think *you* are lying."

"No, sir," said Amelia Bedelia.

"You are a lion. I am Amelia Bedelia."

"Arrrrrgggggh!" roared Mr. Lyon.

The phone went *click*.

CLICK!

"Oh, well," said Amelia Bedelia.

"That lion was not much help at all.

Next time I'll ask for Mr. Tiger."

The kitten still looked hungry.

"Come along," said Amelia Bedelia.

"Let's go do our shopping.

Maybe I can find you something

to eat at the store."

87

She tucked Tiger into her purse,

locked the door, and headed into town.

Along the way Amelia Bedelia

met a letter carrier delivering packages.

"Good afternoon," he said.

"It looks like you are delivering cats."

"Oh, no," said Amelia Bedelia.

"I am trying to deliver lunch

to this hungry kitten."

"You are in luck," said the letter carrier.

"A new fish market just opened.

All cats love to eat fish."

"Where is it?" said Amelia Bedelia.

"You can't miss it," he said.

"Just follow your nose."

"Thank you," said Amelia Bedelia.

As she walked she said to herself,

"Those are very strange directions.

I follow my nose everywhere I go,

unless I walk backward."

Amelia Bedelia strolled by Mrs. Wagner's house.

Her yard was filled with all sorts of things.

"Hi, Amelia Bedelia," said Mrs. Wagner.

"Come and take a look at my garage sale."

"No thanks," said Amelia Bedelia.

"I do not need to buy a garage.

But do you have anything for cats?"

"I did," said Mrs. Wagner.

"I just sold a litter box."

"What is that?" asked Amelia Bedelia.

"Every cat needs one," said Mrs. Wagner.

"That is where a cat goes

   when it needs to go."

"Go where?" said Amelia Bedelia.

"Where would Tiger have to go?"

"Go to the bathroom," said Mrs. Wagner.

"Oh," said Amelia Bedelia. "I see.

   Where would I find a litter box?"

"Let me think," said Mrs. Wagner.

"You might find one at a flea market."

Amelia Bedelia thanked Mrs. Wagner.

She kept walking toward town.

"I would not go to a flea market," she said.

"I do not want Tiger to get fleas."

Finally, Amelia Bedelia and Tiger

arrived in town.

"Look, Tiger," said Amelia Bedelia.

"We are in luck. Here is an empty box

and lots of litter, and it is all free!"

She set the box on the ground.

She filled it up with litter.

She put Tiger in the box.

"You do not look very happy," she said.

"I am not happy," said a voice behind her.

Amelia Bedelia turned around.

A policeman stood there.

He looked very annoyed and said,

"Lady, what do you think you're doing?"

"I am all done," said Amelia Bedelia.

"I made a litter box for Tiger."

"You made a mess," said the policeman.

"Pick that up or I will give you a ticket."

Amelia Bedelia tossed the litter back in the bin.

"Thank you," said the policeman.

"Please do not break any more laws."

"I try not to break things," said Amelia Bedelia.

She and Tiger walked on.

Tiger found the fish market first.

He sniffed the air and licked his whiskers.

Amelia Bedelia walked up to the man selling fish.

"Excuse me," she said.

"Could you spare some scraps for my kitten?"

"You bet," said the man.

He put some fish on a plate.

Tiger devoured the snack.

"He sure likes it," said Amelia Bedelia.

"He certainly does," said the man.

"He is as happy as a clam."

Amelia Bedelia picked up a clam and said,

"They do not look very happy to me."

The man took the clam from her.

He took out a marker

and drew a face on the clam.

"Hold it like this," he said.

"See? That is its smile."

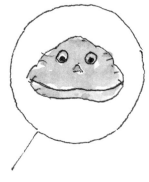

"Now that is one happy clam,"

said Amelia Bedelia.

She laughed and looked down at Tiger.

Tiger had followed a butterfly into the street.

"Watch out!" screamed Amelia Bedelia.

A big truck screeched to a stop.

HONNNNNNK!

Tiger dashed to the sidewalk.

He was so scared

that he scooted up a tree.

The driver got out of his truck to make sure

that he had not hurt the cat.

"Stay put, Tiger,"

said Amelia Bedelia.

"I will rescue you."

Amelia Bedelia started to climb the tree.

"Be careful," said the driver.

"Do not go out on a limb."

"I've got to save my cat,"

yelled Amelia Bedelia.

As she reached out to grab Tiger,

Amelia Bedelia slipped off the branch.

"Whoops!" she said.

"Hang on!" said the driver.

"I will rescue both of you.

I'll get a ladder from my truck."

Amelia Bedelia held on tightly.

Tiger climbed onto her bonnet.

Then Amelia Bedelia saw a familiar car

driving up the street.

"Amelia Bedelia!" said Mrs. Rogers.

"What on earth are you doing?"

"Hanging on," said Amelia Bedelia.

"I wish I were back on earth right now."

Mrs. Rogers drove her car

directly under Amelia Bedelia.

"Let go of the branch," she called out.

Amelia Bedelia and Tiger

dropped onto the roof of the car.

Mrs. Rogers and the driver

helped Amelia Bedelia

and Tiger get down.

Amelia Bedelia tucked Tiger

back into her purse.

"Please, miss," said the driver,

"do not let that cat out of the bag again."

"I won't," said Amelia Bedelia.

"Not until we get home."

101

Mrs. Rogers, Amelia Bedelia, and Tiger

got into the car and drove away.

"Good thing I ran into you," said Mrs. Rogers.

"I gave you a lift and did not drop you at all."

"You are right," said Amelia Bedelia.

She told Mrs. Rogers how she found Tiger

and tried to take care of him.

"In that case," said Mrs. Rogers,

"we should stop right here."

She pulled over to the curb suddenly.

"This is a very good pet store,"

said Mrs. Rogers.

"We can find everything you need

to take good care of your cat."

"Thank you so much," said Amelia Bedelia.

The clerk helped Mrs. Rogers gather

everything they would need,

including a litter box.

Tiger had his eye on a toy.

"You know," said Amelia Bedelia,

"I had better walk Tiger home

before he gets into any more trouble.

The house is just a few blocks away."

"See you there," said Mrs. Rogers.

By the time Amelia Bedelia

and Tiger got back home,

they were both exhausted.

Amelia Bedelia sat down.

She took off her bonnet,

and Tiger curled up in it.

The inside was soft and warm.

Tiger purred once.

A second later, he was snoozing.

"Good idea," said Amelia Bedelia.

"I will close my eyes, too, for a minute."

She put her feet up and leaned back.

Twenty minutes later,

Mr. Rogers came home.

"Well, well," said Mr. Rogers.

"Look what the cat dragged in."

Amelia Bedelia woke up with a start.

"I am sorry," said Amelia Bedelia.

"I must have dozed off."

"Don't worry," said Mr. Rogers.

"Catnaps are nice, especially with a cat."

Amelia Bedelia introduced Mr. Rogers to Tiger.

"Say," asked Mr. Rogers,

"where is Mrs. Rogers?"

"The last time I saw her,"

said Amelia Bedelia,

"she was in the pet store."

"Oh, really,"

said Mr. Rogers.

"My wife was in the pet store?

How much did they

want for her?"

Mr. Rogers began to chuckle.

Just then, Mrs. Rogers stormed in.

"I heard that!" she said.

"Just kidding, my pet," said Mr. Rogers.

He helped her with her packages.

"Is all this for the cat?" he asked.

"Yes it is," said Mrs. Rogers.

"I should have gotten you a collar,

since you are now in the doghouse."

Mr. Rogers was not laughing now.

"Just kidding, my pet," said Mrs. Rogers.

They leaned over together to look at Tiger.

"Who meowed?" said Amelia Bedelia.

"Don't look at me," said Mr. Rogers.

MEOW

They all turned around.

A large cat sat outside the window.

It looked like Tiger, but bigger.

MEOW-MEOW-MEEEEOWww!

Tiger sprang onto the windowsill.

Both cats were happy to see each other.

"How sweet," said Mrs. Rogers.

"That cat must be his mother."

Amelia Bedelia let Tiger outside.

The big cat licked Tiger twice,

then picked him up in her mouth.

She headed across the yard.

"Stop!" shouted Amelia Bedelia.

"That big cat is eating my kitten!"

"No it isn't," said Mr. Rogers.

"That is how a mother cat

moves her babies from place to place."

They all ran after the cat.

Down the street, a moving van

was parked in front of a house.

A little girl stood in the front yard.

"What's going on?" said Amelia Bedelia.

"Is this another garage sale?"

The cat dropped Tiger into a box.

"There you are!" said the girl.

"Is that your cat?" asked Amelia Bedelia.

"Yes, it is," said the girl.

"Her name is Muffin.

My name is Sarah."

They all introduced themselves to Sarah.

Then they looked into the box.

Tiger was playing

with his brothers and sisters.

Sarah hugged Amelia Bedelia and said,

"Thanks for finding my kitten."

"My pleasure," said Amelia Bedelia.

"Is this a litter box?"

Sarah laughed. "No," she said.

"This isn't her litter box,

but this is her litter.

Muffin had kittens a month ago."

Amelia Bedelia shook her head,

shrugged her shoulders, and said,

"I still have a lot to learn about cats."

Big drops of rain began to fall.

"Uh-oh," said Mr. Rogers.

"The weatherman guessed right for once."

"Bye-bye, Sarah," said Amelia Bedelia.

"Come back tomorrow," said Sarah.

They ran back home in a downpour.

Mr. and Mrs. Rogers went inside.

Amelia Bedelia stayed out on the porch.

She looked at the rain and said to herself,

"The weather forecast was half right.

Today it only rained cats."

A tail was sticking out from behind a tree.

"Jeepers!" said Amelia Bedelia.

"A tree just barked at me."

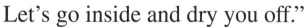

A puppy peeked out

from behind the trunk.

It ran onto the porch

and jumped into Amelia Bedelia's arms.

"Hi there," she said. "You are soaked.

Let's go inside and dry you off."

Amelia Bedelia opened the door

and called out:

"Yoo-hoo, Mr. Rogers—

I found the other half

of the weather forecast.

Now you'll have company

in the doghouse!"

Amelia Bedelia's All Mixed Up!

Amelia Bedelia is all mixed up! Help her by unscrambling these words. (Hint: Use the pictures to help you figure out the words.)

R I E T G

tiger

T C A S

cats

E W M O

meow

O T E R M H

mother

Spot the Difference

These two pictures are not
exactly the same.
Five things from picture #1
are missing from picture #2.
Can you spot them?

Two Ways to Say It!

Amelia Bedelia always takes things literally, and that leads to funny misunderstandings. Here are some confusing expressions from *Amelia Bedelia and the Cat*. Can you think of any other words or expressions Amelia Bedelia misunderstands in this story?

It is going to rain cats and dogs!

It is going to rain really hard!

"Why don't I give you a lift and drop you in town?"

"I can give you a ride to town in my car."

He is as happy as a clam.

He is completely contented.

Tiger's Maze

Help the lost kitten pick the path that leads to his mother and brothers and sisters.

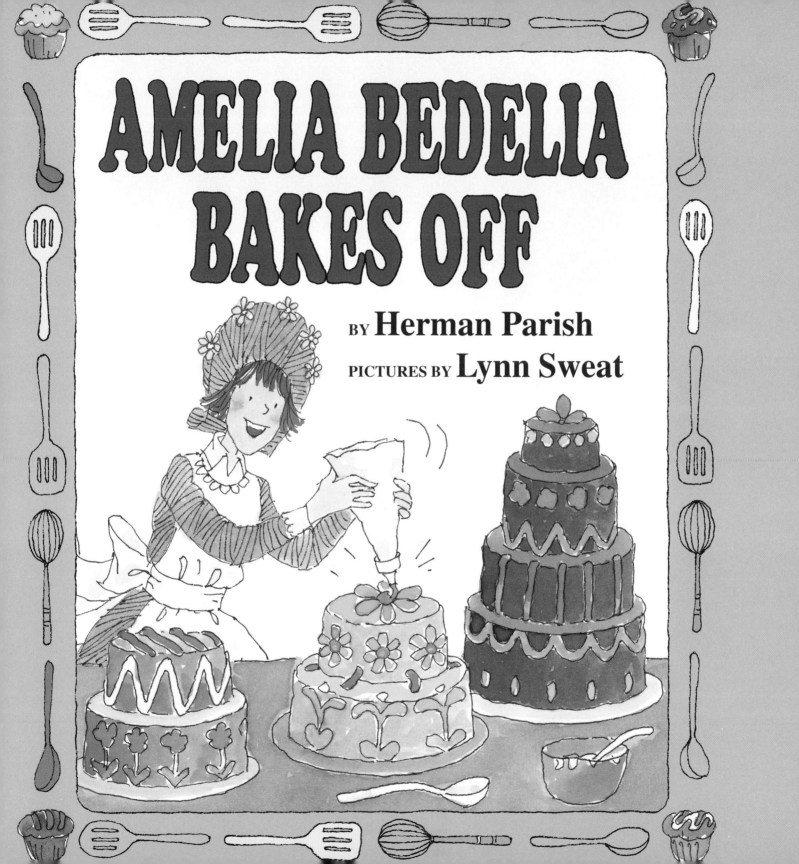

AMELIA BEDELIA BAKES OFF

BY **Herman Parish**

PICTURES BY **Lynn Sweat**

On her day off, Amelia Bedelia

stopped by to visit Mr. and Mrs. Rogers.

"Morning, everybody," said Amelia Bedelia.

"Shhhhh!" said Mr. Rogers.

"Sorry," said Amelia Bedelia quietly.

"Don't mind him," said Mrs. Rogers.

"He's watching his favorite show,

What's Cooking?"

"I give up," said Amelia Bedelia.

"What are you cooking?"

"Nothing," said Mrs. Rogers.

"That is the name of the program."

Mr. Rogers was getting annoyed.

"Please be quiet, for Pete's sake!"

"Who is Pete?"

Amelia Bedelia whispered.

Mrs. Rogers smiled and said,

"His name is Chef Du Jour.

He shows people how to make

gourmet meals and fancy desserts."

Mr. Rogers turned up the volume.

"Don't forget!"

Chef Du Jour was saying.

"I'll pick the winner

of my big Bake-Off contest.

The best baker will get

one thousand dollars!"

The audience applauded wildly.

Mr. Rogers clapped his hands, too.

"Wow!" he said. "A thousand bucks!

That is a lot of dough!"

"Not really," said Amelia Bedelia.

"A thousand bucks is a lot of deer,

but there is no doe at all."

"Amelia Bedelia," said Mrs. Rogers,

"you ought to enter that contest.

You make the best lemon meringue pie."

"She's right," said Mr. Rogers.

"A smart cookie would give it a try."

"Thanks anyway," said Amelia Bedelia.

"By tonight I will be all baked out.

Cousin Alcolu and I are running

Grace's Cookie Jar all day today."

"You two, run a bakery?" said Mr. Rogers.

"That sounds like a half-baked idea."

"No it isn't," said Amelia Bedelia.

"This idea is completely baked.

Grace had to go out of town.

She left us her recipes."

"You'll do fine," said Mrs. Rogers.

"Call us if you need help."

"Will do," said Amelia Bedelia.

On her way to the bakery, Amelia Bedelia

thought about smart cookies.

Did they taste better?

By the time she arrived,

Cousin Alcolu was unlocking the door.

"Hi, Cousin Alcolu," said Amelia Bedelia.

"Hey there," he said. "You look puzzled."

"I was wondering," said Amelia Bedelia.

"Can a cookie be smart?"

Cousin Alcolu shrugged his shoulders.

"A cookie can be rich," he said.

"I've heard that, too," she said.

"Is that what a fortune cookie is?"

Cousin Alcolu shrugged again and said,

"Maybe so. We'd better get started."

They went inside and got ready

to do some serious baking.

They found a big stack of recipes,

along with a note from Grace.

"This will be easy," said Amelia Bedelia.

"Grace will tell us exactly what to do."

They read her note together.

START EVERY
RECIPE
FROM
SCRATCH!

grace

Amelia Bedelia scratched

Cousin Alcolu's back.

Then Cousin Alcolu

scratched her back.

"That felt good," said Amelia Bedelia.

"Now I feel like baking. What's first?"

Cousin Alcolu read from the note aloud:

"Bake a batch of chocolate chip cookies,

but cut the recipe in half."

"That's easy," said Amelia Bedelia.

Cousin Alcolu shook his head.

"You know," said Amelia Bedelia,

"I guess we ought to cut all of the

chocolate chips in half, too."

"What?" said Cousin Alcolu.

"That will take forever!"

"I know, I know," said Amelia Bedelia.

"But we'd better follow Grace's instructions,

or the cookies may not turn out so tasty."

She began to cut each chip in half.

Bits of chocolate flew everywhere.

"This is so silly," said Cousin Alcolu.

"These are not very smart cookies."

"Not smart is right," said Amelia Bedelia.

"These are definitely dumb cookies."

Amelia Bedelia looked at Grace's recipes.

"Gosh," she said. "This is unbelievable.

Grace wants us to bake twelve pound cakes."

"Are you sure?" said Cousin Alcolu.

"Twelve pounds is a mighty heavy cake.

How many twelve-pound cakes

does Grace want us to bake?"

"She didn't say," said Amelia Bedelia.

"Her recipe is for just one pound cake.

One twelve-pound cake should be plenty."

Cousin Alcolu scratched his head.

"Hmmmm," he said.

"If we bake twelve one-pound cakes,

then stack them on top of one another . . ."

"That's it!" said Amelia Bedelia.

"That adds up to a twelve-pound cake.

Cousin Alcolu, you are a genius."

Amelia Bedelia found twelve pans.

She mixed up a huge bowl of batter.

It was enough for thirteen cakes.

She found another pan and crammed

all thirteen cakes into the oven to bake.

"You know," said Cousin Alcolu,

"a 'baker's dozen' is actually thirteen."

"See there," said Amelia Bedelia.

"You can count better than a baker."

Cousin Alcolu finished cutting

all of the chocolate chips in half.

Then he read the other half of the recipe.

"Please bring me the salt," he said.

"Here you go," said Amelia Bedelia.

She brought him a huge box of salt.

"That is too much," said Cousin Alcolu.

"I just need a pinch."

Amelia Bedelia reached out and . . .

"Ouch!" hollered Cousin Alcolu.

"What did you pinch me for?"

"For the recipe," said Amelia Bedelia.

"I gave you a pinch, like you asked."

Cousin Alcolu rubbed his arm.

"I'm so sorry," said Amelia Bedelia.

"I didn't mean to hurt you.

Now you've got a chip on your shoulder."

"No, I don't," said Cousin Alcolu.

"I'd never hold a grudge against you."

"Hold still," said Amelia Bedelia.

She reached out and plucked

a chocolate chip off his shoulder.

Then she said, "Open wide!"

She tossed the chip into his mouth.

"Yum!" said Cousin Alcolu. "Thanks!"

He finished mixing the dough

and put a batch of cookies

into the second oven to bake.

Amelia Bedelia got three cakes

out of the refrigerator.

"What are those?" asked Cousin Alcolu.

"Grace calls them 'cheesecakes,'"

said Amelia Bedelia.

"We're supposed to put cherries on top."

"Cherries with cheese?" said Cousin Alcolu.

"Sounds like a yucky combination to me."

"Me, too," said Amelia Bedelia.

"I bet if these cakes looked cheesier,

they wouldn't need any cherries."

They cut holes

to make a Swiss cheese cake,

drizzled food coloring

to paint a blue cheese cake,

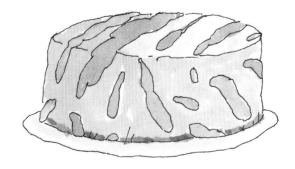

and planted flags to create

an American cheese cake.

Just then, the oven timer went off.

Amelia Bedelia and Cousin Alcolu

took out the pound cakes

and put them on racks to cool.

Then they took the cookies out of the oven

and had a tea break to sample them.

"You know what?" said Amelia Bedelia.

"They taste better with the chips cut in half.

  These are smart cookies after all."

"It was worth the work," said Cousin Alcolu.

"Now let's build that twelve-pound cake."

Amelia Bedelia handed him cake after cake.

Cousin Alcolu carefully stacked each one

higher and higher and higher.

"Is it my imagination," said Amelia Bedelia,

"or are the cakes starting to lean?"

"I can't tell," said Cousin Alcolu.

"Hand me that last cake, please."

As soon as he put it on top,

it slid off and crashed onto the table.

"Uh-oh," said Cousin Alcolu.

"This pound cake got pounded."

"No problem," said Amelia Bedelia.

"Our baker's dozen gave us a spare cake.

 Bakers must know that accidents happen."

"Lucky for us," said Cousin Alcolu.

Amelia Bedelia checked the recipes.

"Hold on," she said. "This is even luckier.

Grace wants us to make a crumb cake.

Let's just press these crumbs together."

The two of them pushed and prodded

until the crumbs turned into a cake.

"Presto—crumb cake!" said Amelia Bedelia.

"Yessiree," said Cousin Alcolu.

"That is one crummy cake!"

"Uh-oh," said Amelia Bedelia.

"Did we leave something in the oven?"

"That's the phone," said Cousin Alcolu.

"Hello," said Amelia Bedelia.

"This is Grace's Cookie Jar.

 May I help you?"

"Hi, it's Grace," said Grace.

"How are things going?"

"Almost done," said Amelia Bedelia.

"We've got one last cake to go,

but I think I'll make it at home."

"Good thinking," said Grace.

"You must be exhausted."

"I am," said Amelia Bedelia.

"I'll bring it in tomorrow."

"I've got an idea," said Grace.

"I'll be at the big Bake-Off.

Just meet me there, okay?"

"Okay," said Amelia Bedelia.

"Thank you! Bye-bye,"

said Grace.

Cousin Alcolu began to clean up.

"I'll handle this mess," he said.

"You go home and bake that cake,

then get some sleep."

"Thank you," said Amelia Bedelia.

"I can barely keep my eyes open."

By the time she got home,

Amelia Bedelia was yawning,

but she had one last cake in her.

It was an old family recipe that

her grandmother had taught her.

There were just nine ingredients.

She mixed them up right in the pan,

then put the pan in the oven.

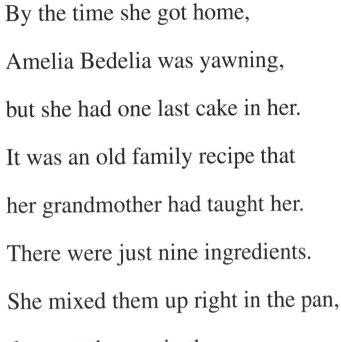

After the cake had baked and cooled,

she cut two tiny pieces off one end

and set them right on top.

Then she frosted and decorated

her cake from top to bottom.

The next day, Amelia Bedelia overslept.

She was tired from all that baking.

She picked up her cake

and dashed to the Bake-Off.

Incredible cakes filled the hall.

Television cameras were everywhere.

Reporters interviewed the bakers.

The excitement was building.

Amelia Bedelia looked around.

She did not see Grace anywhere.

Amelia Bedelia put her cake down on a table

and went to search for her.

At that moment, Chef Du Jour

strolled in Amelia Bedelia's direction.

He looked grumpy, just like on TV.

When he got to Amelia Bedelia's cake,

Chef Du Jour stopped in his tracks.

"What is this?" asked Chef Du Jour.

"Is this someone's idea of a joke?"

"It's my idea,"

  said Amelia Bedelia.

"And it is no joke."

"Then what is it?"

  demanded the chef.

"It started out as a sheet cake,"

said Amelia Bedelia.

"But I was so tired when I baked it,

I went ahead and made the whole bed."

A smile came over the chef's face.

"It's so easy to make,"

  said Amelia Bedelia.

"And it's pretty tasty."

"Really?" said the chef.

"You can actually eat it?"

"Here," said Amelia Bedelia.

"Bite into a pillow."

  The chef took a bite.

  He closed his eyes and

  his smile got even bigger.

"Your cake is simple," he said,

"yet the flavor is complex.

It's funny, but seriously delicious."

"Glad you like it," said Amelia Bedelia.

"Like it?" said Chef Du Jour.

"I love it!

It's fantastic!

Your cake takes the cake,

and first prize!"

There was a huge cheer.

Amelia Bedelia smiled

and waved to everyone at home,

especially the two she knew were watching.

Mr. and Mrs. Rogers were speechless.

Then they jumped for joy.

"See there," said Mrs. Rogers.

"Amelia Bedelia is a smart cookie after all."

"She sure is," said Mr. Rogers.

"And with a thousand dollars,

she's a fortune cookie, too!"

Amelia Bedelia's Sheet Cake

3 cups flour

1 ¾ cups sugar

2 teaspoons baking soda

1 teaspoon salt

⅔ cup cocoa

¾ cup vegetable oil

2 tablespoons vinegar

1 teaspoon vanilla

2 cups water

Step 1

Sift the flour, sugar, baking soda, salt, and cocoa directly into an ungreased 9″ x 13″ pan. Add oil, vinegar, and vanilla. Pour water over all ingredients. Mix with a fork until smooth.

Step 2

Bake at 350 degrees for 25 to 30 minutes.

Step 3

Cool the cake and ice it in the pan with your favorite frosting.

Help Amelia Bedelia Find Her Cake

Find Amelia Bedelia's Shadow

Have you read these other stories about Amelia Bedelia?

I Can Read! 2
Amelia Bedelia
by Peggy Parish • pictures by Fritz Siebel

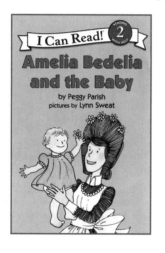

I Can Read! 2
Amelia Bedelia and the Baby
by Peggy Parish
pictures by Lynn Sweat

I Can Read! 2
Play Ball, Amelia Bedelia
by Peggy Parish • pictures by Wallace Tripp

I Can Read! 2
Amelia Bedelia and the Surprise Shower
by Peggy Parish • pictures by Barbara Siebel Thomas

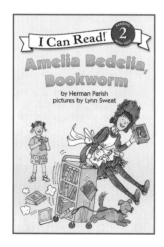

I Can Read! 2
Amelia Bedelia, Bookworm
by Herman Parish
pictures by Lynn Sweat

I Can Read! 2
Amelia Bedelia Under Construction
by Herman Parish
pictures by Lynn Sweat

I Can Read! 2
Amelia Bedelia, Rocket Scientist?
by Herman Parish
pictures by Lynn Sweat

I Can Read! 2
Amelia Bedelia, Cub Reporter
by Herman Parish
pictures by Lynn Sweat

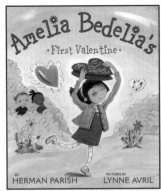

Amelia Bedelia's · First Day of School · BY HERMAN PARISH PICTURES BY LYNNE AVRIL

Amelia Bedelia's · First Valentine · BY HERMAN PARISH PICTURES BY LYNNE AVRIL

Amelia Bedelia's · First Apple Pie · BY HERMAN PARISH PICTURES BY LYNNE AVRIL

Amelia Bedelia's · First Field Trip · BY HERMAN PARISH PICTURES BY LYNNE AVRIL

Discover these books about Amelia Bedelia's childhood adventures!

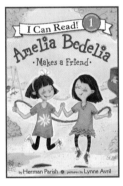

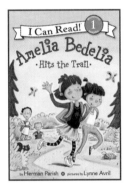
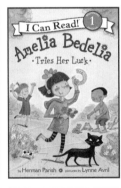

I Can Read! 1 — Amelia Bedelia · Makes a Friend · by Herman Parish pictures by Lynne Avril

I Can Read! 1 — Amelia Bedelia · Sleeps Over · by Herman Parish pictures by Lynne Avril

I Can Read! 1 — Amelia Bedelia · Hits the Trail · by Herman Parish pictures by Lynne Avril

I Can Read! 1 — Amelia Bedelia · Tries Her Luck · by Herman Parish pictures by Lynne Avril

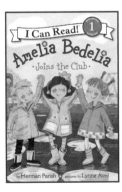

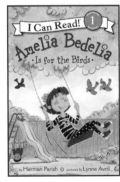

I Can Read! 1 — Amelia Bedelia · Joins the Club · by Herman Parish pictures by Lynne Avril

I Can Read! 1 — Amelia Bedelia · Chalks One Up · by Herman Parish pictures by Lynne Avril

I Can Read! 1 — Amelia Bedelia · Is for the Birds · by Herman Parish pictures by Lynne Avril

I Can Read! 1 — Amelia Bedelia · By the Yard · YARD SALE BUY THE YARD · by Herman Parish pictures by Lynne Avril

Answer Key

p. 68: TONGUE, EGG, NOSE, ICE CREAM

p. 69: Circles mark things that are missing from picture #2

p. 120: TIGER, CATS, MEOW, MOTHER

p. 121: Circles mark things that are missing from picture #2

p. 123: Tiger found his way through the maze!: Path 2

p. 188: Amelia Bedelia found her cake!

p. 189: Amelia Bedelia's real shadow is C.